Murder in the Highlands

Penelope Sotheby

Copyright © 2018 Penelope Sotheby

First published in 2018 by Jonmac Limited.

All rights reserved.

This book is a work of fiction. All names, characters and places, incidents are used entirely fictitiously. Any resemblance to actual events, or persons, living or dead, is entirely coincidental.

No part of this publication may be reproduced, or transmitted in any form or by any means, electronic or otherwise, without written permission from the publisher.

Free Book

Sign up for this author's new release mailing list and receive a free copy of her very first novella *Murder At The Inn*. This fantastic whodunit will keep you guessing to the very end and is not currently available anywhere else.

Go to http://fantasticfiction.info/murder-at-the-inn/ to have a look.

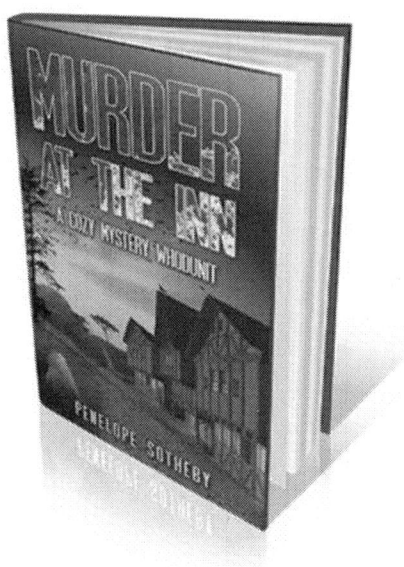

Other Books By The Author

Murder at the Inn

Murder on the Village Green (A Diane Dimbleby Cozy Mystery)

Murder in the Neighbourhood (A Diane Dimbleby Cozy Mystery)

Murder on a Yacht (A Diane Dimbleby Cozy Mystery)

Murder in the Village (A Diane Dimbleby Cozy Mystery)

Murder in the Mail (A Diane Dimbleby Cozy Mystery)

Murder in the Development (A Diane Dimbleby Cozy Mystery)

Table of Contents

Free Book iii

Other Books By The Author iv

Chapter 1 1

Chapter 2 13

Chapter 3 33

Chapter 4 39

Chapter 5 49

Chapter 6 57

Chapter 7 67

Chapter 8 75

Chapter 9 81

Chapter 10 85

Get Your Free Copy of "Murder at the Inn" 103

Other Books by This Author 105

About The Author 111

Fantastic Fiction 113

Chapter 1

Diane Dimbleby was positively excited, as excited as an English woman could get at her age. At the age of 61 however, she was not at all certain that excitement was a good idea. Resolving to contain her excitement, she leaned on the railing of the ferry and enjoyed the feeling of the sun on her face and the wind in her hair. She closed her eyes and was temporarily lost in the moment.

The moment passed surprisingly fast. Diane remembered that she had neglected to put on sunscreen and her gray, blunt cut bob was surely a tangled mess by now. She looked around the ferry and realized that she was the only person outside. The other tourists were far too busy texting and playing games on their phones in the air-conditioned convenience of the passengers' lounge.

She was convinced that she must look a fright and returned to the comfort of her Land Rover parked nearby on deck. She opened the car door and was temporarily caught off guard by a powerful gust of wind that tried to snatch the door out of her hand. She smiled and remembered that the weather in the Highlands of Scotland could be unpredictable even in summer. She slid into the passenger's side seat and closed the door, then flipped the mirror down and took a good look at herself.

Aside from the mess of gray hair that needed a bit of brushing, she was pleased by the reflection. Her bright blue eyes sparkled, and she still had a lovely peaches and cream complexion. She found her purse and dug around until she had located the hairbrush. She tamed her unruly tresses and looked back at her reflection. Her hair was in place, and she looked much more like the retired school teacher she was accustomed to seeing in the mirror back home in Apple Mews.

She flipped the mirror back into place and located the laptop bag in the back seat. She decided to take advantage of the 6-mile ferry ride to the Isle of Skye and try to get some work done on her latest murder mystery. With her purse on her shoulder and her laptop bag in her hand, she climbed out of the Land Rover, clicked the button on the key fob to lock it and made her way to the passenger lounge.

The heavy door was no match for the wind whipping around her light jacket as she walked into the lounge. The tables were full of young families, bored teenagers, newlyweds and retired couples. She looked for an open space at a table and was fortunate that one remained in the corner by the drink machine and the kettle. She quickly walked down the narrow aisle and claimed the last remaining table before anyone else realized it was free.

Diane tucked her hair behind her ears and unpacked her laptop. She switched the power on and looked at the battery life; four hours, it cheerfully glowed. 1 hour and 20 minutes would be plenty of time. The ferry normally only took 1 hour to arrive at the Isle of Skye from the ferry port at Mallaig.

She unpacked her tiny set of earbuds and plugged them into the jack on the side of the laptop. She located the saved playlist on the music files and found the one labeled Scotland. She hovered the cursor over the playlist and clicked play.

In only a matter of seconds, Diane was transported to a Broadway version of the Highlands. Brigadoon played in her earbuds, and she smiled as she heard the overture. It was corny, but she always associated Brigadoon with the town of Portree on Skye. She knew she would be embarrassed if anyone should happen to find out about this guilty musical pleasure, but it made her happy, and that was all that mattered.

Skye was one of her favorite places to holiday. Each year she tried to spend at least one week on this island in the Scottish Highlands. She closed her eyes and envisioned the waterfront of Portree with its row of colorful houses, shops, and restaurants. She could imagine the beautiful Quiraing and the majestic Cuillins.

As she listened to the melodic strains of the songs from the musical, she thought about Glen Gorm Hotel. It was only a short distance from the village of Armadale, yet it felt as though it existed in its own little world. The Victorian house was really a small castle and had been built on the rocky coast overlooking the sea. The estate at the Glen Gorm Hotel was breathtakingly scenic with nature walks, a coffee shop, and a wildlife tour.

Staying at the hotel was one of her favorite ways to relax and to unwind. The rooms were always spacious and affordable, the food positively delectable and the guests at the hotel always interesting. She never failed to meet people at the hotel that served as inspirations for characters for her books. She clicked on the word processing program on her laptop and remembered that although she was on holiday, she really should be writing.

She clicked her saved document and opened up the file. For a while she stared at the blue screen of the computer and realized that she was absolutely drawing a blank. She was writing a murder mystery, and she was at a critical place in the plot. Then she realized that she was much too distracted at present to work on her novel.

Visions of eagles soaring through the air on a morning nature walk followed by crisp butter scones for tea were distracting her from the hour she should be putting to good use.

Diane looked at the blinking cursor on the blank page of the laptop and felt as though it was taunting her. She clicked on the pause button on the music player and removed the earbuds from her ears, then unzipped her purse and pulled out her wallet. She walked the four steps to the vending machine and put a few coins in the slot.

After selecting a box of chocolate biscuits, which slid into the chute with an audible thud, she put her hand in the door and hoped that not too many biscuits had been obliterated by their sudden encounter with gravity. Biscuits and wallet in hand, she went to the kettle and was pleased that there was hot water still in it. She selected a boring but reliable orange pekoe blended tea bag and poured the hot water into a Styrofoam cup, before walking the few steps back to her table.

Diane checked her phone to see if her husband Albert had called. He was visiting his sister in Taunton and so it was this that prompted Diane to take a long overdue trip north. Albert's sister, although friendly towards Diane, never fully took to her for some reason and so Diane made her excuses and decided to do her own thing. Seeing that he did not call, Diane made a note that she would email him later. Obtaining a cell phone signal could not always be guaranteed where she was going to, but this did not bother Diane too much. At the very least it meant that Inspector Darrel Crothers could not call her about some incident or other in her home town of Apple Mews.

Steam rose from the cup; it was not perfect, but at least it was hot. Even on a summer's day in July, there was something reassuring about a fresh cup of tea and a biscuit. She sat back down, this time without the distraction of music. She clicked on her word processing program and started a new document. The blank page opened and with a sudden burst of inspiration she began typing at a furious pace, filling the page with an in-depth description of her destination.

She wrote about Skye, the shops in Portree, the Glen Gorm Hotel and her friends, the real reason she had driven all this way from Apple Mews, Shropshire. She changed their names and a few key details about the proprietors of the Glen Gorm Hotel, and found that even writing about this lively and amicable couple made her smile.

Her fingers sped over the keys of her laptop as she described the Glen Gorm Hotel. The Victorian house was much too large to really be considered a house. It had over a dozen bedrooms, several guest cottages, and a coffee shop on the premises. The present owners Juliana and Malcolm MacKay had spent a small fortune refurbishing it and outfitting it with the luxuries and modern conveniences, while still retaining the charm of a small castle in the Highlands.

Diane thought about the attention to detail that Juliana and Malcolm had insisted the contractors take with every aspect of the restoration. Each wood panel, piece of furniture and tea cup were lovingly restored or replaced so that visitors would be transported back to an idyllic era of gracious living and days spent in pursuit of leisurely activities. The effect of the restoration was stunning. Diane always felt relaxed from the moment her car turned onto the gravel road leading to the hotel.

Glen Gorm had originally belonged to Malcolm's grandmother and had been in his family since it was built back in the 1870s. His grandmother had suffered terribly from dementia, and the house had fallen into a state of disrepair during the last few years of her life. Diane wrote about Malcolm and Juliana's dedication to his grandmother. She described how they had worked tirelessly while his grandmother was still living to keep the house in habitable condition.

Diane knew that Malcolm had been working as a doctor in Inverness while his grandmother was still alive and admired Malcolm and Juliana's dedication to the grandmother. Not a weekend went by in good weather or rough that they did not try to come out to Glen Gorm to check in on her. It was a heartwarming tale she thought, as she typed their story onto the digital page and into her computer's memory.

Yes, it was a touching tale, but so too was the story of how they had met. She smiled and reached for her tea. Steam was still rising from the cup as she tentatively took a sip. It was quite hot but drinkable. She sipped the warm amber liquid and put the cup back on the table, then opened the box of biscuits and removed one from the package. She bit into the chocolate biscuit and thought about the story that her friend Juliana had shared with her several years ago.

Juliana had told her about how she had met Malcolm. Juliana was still a university student on holiday vacationing in the Highlands with her parents. They had been on the Isle of Skye and had stopped in Portree with a tour group. There was a choice of either shopping on the main street, or a guided birdwatching tour was on the itinerary that day. Juliana's parents had chosen go shopping; Juliana, being the outdoorsy type, had decided to go bird watching. She was the youngest person on the tour; well, almost the youngest, because the young man leading the tour was Malcolm. He worked as a tour guide during the summer holidays to make a little extra money while he was at university. Of course, Diane always thought that he would have eagerly shared his extensive knowledge of his home for free.

Diane remembered Juliana was impressed with his knowledge not only of the avian population, but the wildlife and the history of the area. From Malcolm's perspective, Diane recalled his astonishment that a beautiful young woman from the bustling metropolis of London was even the slightest bit interested in the natural beauty of his small corner of the world. The town of Portree was so small compared to London that he could not imagine how she was not bored to pieces, but then Juliana was no ordinary girl. It was truly love at first sight.

They had been together ever since, all through his years in medical school, his work in Inverness and finally, after his grandmother's death ten years ago, they had retired to Glen Gorm and opened the castle as a hotel. It had been a great success, and they were a wonderful couple. Diane had met them on holiday a few years back, and now she no longer considered them the proprietors of her favorite hotel, but truly considered them to be friends.

Diane typed their story and her thoughts on the small town of Portree. She had never before considered using the Isle of Skye and the Glen Gorm Hotel as a backdrop to one of her stories. She decided that it was such a lovely place and their story was so romantic that it might give her inspiration to write a romance novel or a nature guide. When she finished typing, she read over her work and saved it.

She clicked on the document that she should have been working on and, feeling inspired by a sudden burst of creativity, began working on her novel again; the muse was back. As she typed details of her latest murder mystery, she thought that the muse had led her to write about the hotel and wondered if she should follow the whims of it.

She drank her now lukewarm tea and kept working until she noticed the tourists all preparing to return to their cars. She packed up her laptop and threw away her trash in the rubbish bin. She slid her purse over her shoulder and returned to her Land Rover. The ferry was slowly pulling up to the dock at Armadale. She buckled her seatbelt and put the key in the ignition. The ferry came to a stop, the ferry boat workers finished the docking procedures, and only a few minutes later, she drove onto the Isle of Skye.

She rolled down the window and took a deep breath of fresh air, which had the salty smell of the ocean. Diane found that smell to be exhilarating. She drove the short distance to the A851 which followed, at least for a while, the eastern coast of the island. It was a scenic view, and she enjoyed the short drive. She never really felt like she was on holiday until she was officially on the island. Now she was here, and she couldn't be happier.

This day was turning out perfect in every way; the weather was warm, the smell of the ocean was on the breeze, and the plants and grass of the island were crisp hues of green under a bright blue sky. She was sure that she must have had a silly smile on her face as she turned off the main road at Kilbeg and onto a narrow road leading the 2 miles to the hotel. She could feel her shoulders relaxing and her disposition becoming more cheerful as she drove closer to the Glen Gorm Hotel.

She was jolted out of her state of bliss and contentment by a police car that suddenly appeared behind her. The lights of the police car were flashing, and for a moment Diane wondered if she had been driving too fast. A quick look at her speedometer told her that was not the case. Just to be certain, she slowed down, and the police car sped around and resumed its quick rate of speed, and was soon around the bend in the road and out of sight.

Her feeling of relief was quickly replaced by a rising sense of alarm. There was only one destination at the end of the road, and that was the Glen Gorm Hotel. The relaxation and contentment that she had just been enjoying were now but a memory. She was not sure why a police car was going to the hotel, but her intuition told her that this morning was no longer perfect.

Chapter 2

She arrived at the hotel minutes later and was greeted by a disconcerting sight. There was an ambulance and several police cars parked at the entrance. Diane wasted no time parking her vehicle and hurrying inside. Although perfectly calm in demeanor, on the inside she was trying to control her fears; she hoped that Malcolm and Juliana were not taken ill.

She walked into the lobby and was greeted by a police officer.

"I am going to have to ask you not to go upstairs."

"Yes sir, I am a personal friend of the owners, is everything okay?"

"Ma'am, I am not at liberty to say. Please have a seat until we can get this sorted."

Diane sat on a beautifully upholstered couch by the fireplace in the great hall. She tried to remain calm and looked for her friends, but did not see either one. In her haste to get inside, she had completely forgotten that she had her cellphone in the pocket of her jacket. She reached into the pocket and powered the phone on. She typed in her passcode and immediately texted Juliana. She hoped that Juliana had her cell phone with her.

She stared at the tiny screen and wished her friend would text her back or call. She felt silly texting her when she could be in the same building, but the police officer was unlikely to let her go roaming to look for her. She was so busy concentrating on the small screen of her cellphone that she was caught by surprise.

"Diane!" exclaimed a tall woman, slightly younger than herself. It was Juliana. Diane was relieved to see her.

"My dear, please tell me that both you and Malcolm are well."

"Yes, we are."

"I hate to pry, but you seem to have all of the police officers on the island at your hotel."

"It does seem that way. Come with me, we can talk in my office."

Juliana led the way down a corridor leading from the great hall to a small but sunny office. Diane followed her into the room and shut the door.

"I am so glad you are here," said Juliana as she hugged Diane, then sat down on the corner of her desk.

"What has happened? Nothing serious, I trust?"

"I'm afraid so. There has been a murder."

"A murder?"

"Yes, it would seem so. One of the guests is dead, and the detective from Inverness believes it to be a murder. I must admit I am beside myself. I don't know what to do."

"There, there, everything will be fine. Where is Malcolm?"

"He is upstairs assisting the Detective; I am supposed to e-mail the details of the guest list to him."

"Do you know what happened?"

"It's Mr. Snelling –Mr. James Snelling. He had stayed at the hotel before." Juliana began to cry.

Diane could tell that the stress and strain of this unfortunate incident had affected Julian's normally calm composure. She found a tissue box on a shelf and handed Juliana a tissue.

"Thank you," said Juliana as she dabbed at her eyes with the tissue, "As I said, it's Mr. Snelling. He died sometime last night. Malcolm had treated him the last time he stayed with us. I am afraid that his heart was not good."

"Did he have a heart attack? A heart attack is not usually murder."

"He did have a heart attack, but there seems to be more to it," said Juliana as she wiped her eyes. "His room, it was vandalized; it looked like a tiger or a great big cat shredded the walls and destroyed the paintings. What is even worse is that no one heard a thing. A man dies, and his room is destroyed, and yet no one heard a single noise, how is that possible?"

"I don't have an answer for you about that, at least not yet."

"I don't know what to think. Do we have a murderer staying at the hotel, a wild animal on the loose? Are we all in danger?" asked Juliana, who was now crying and on the verge of becoming hysterical.

"Juliana, I know this is overwhelming, but try to pull yourself together. We need to decide what the safest course of action is. We have to be strong."

"Diane, you are right. We all have to be strong."

Diane and Juliana left the oasis of tranquility that was the study. Julia's eyes were still a bit puffy, but she looked as though she might weather the storm after all. Diane concluded that all Julia needed was a good cry and a sympathetic ear to calm her nerves.

After all, it wasn't an everyday occurrence that one's hotel was crawling with police officers, stressed and fearful guests and possibly a murderer. It was quite easy to understand how one could be stressed and tearful at a time like this. Diane was suitably impressed that her friend was handling the immense pressure as well as she was. It said quite a lot about her character and her mettle.

Upon returning to the great hall, Juliana was immediately surrounded by nervous guests. Diane wondered if leaving the study was such a good idea after all. At least in the study they had the option of locking the door, but regrettably, they could not hide there forever. Juliana looked completely overwhelmed. She was peppered with questions.

"What is the meaning of this? Are we not allowed to leave?"

"I need to get to my room, why am I not allowed to go up?"

"I expect a refund, I did not pay to get involved in anything so sordid, when can I expect my money back?"

Diane stepped in immediately and nodded to Juliana. Juliana excused herself and made a dash for it. The police officer who stood sentry at the staircase permitted her to pass. Juliana turned to look at Diane and mouthed, "Thank you," as she rushed up the stairs.

Diane cleared her throat. "Alright everyone, may I have your attention? This situation is unexpected and regrettably still an ongoing investigation. I assure you that as soon as the police are finished with the preliminaries you will have access to your rooms. As to when you may leave the premises, that is not up to the proprietors but to the police. I am certain the MacKays will want to handle any refunds or discounts personally as soon they can. I can promise you that they will take into account any and all inconvenience or discomfort that you may have suffered due to this unfortunate event."

"Since every police officer on the island is here, does that mean we have a murderer on the loose?" asked a woman who looked around at the other guests nervously.

The other guests nodded their heads and joined in.

"Yes, that's a damn good question, is there a killer on the prowl?"

"Are we safe?"

Diane detected a faint hint of panic beginning to grip the guests. "Everyone pull yourselves together. I am quite certain that you are all safe. The hotel is currently hosting all of the island's police force, and I would wager one or two from Inverness, so at the moment you are quite possibly the safest group of hotel guests on the planet."

"But who is the murderer? Is it one of us?"

Diane answered, "Let the police complete their investigation. As soon as they are finished and have a clearer picture of what may have happened, then I am sure you will find all of your fears unfounded. Now please take a seat in the great hall, the library or the dining room. I will have tea brought out, and there is a drinks cabinet in the library if you find that you need more substantial means to endure the wait."

Diane went to the kitchen and was pleased to find that it had not been quarantined as part of the police investigation. She requested that Mrs. Allan, the hotel cook, see about a pot of tea and sandwiches for the guests. She found in her experience that people endured anything better with a good strong cup of tea. Naturally, the sandwiches never hurt. It always amazed her how much like children adults could be sometimes. A bit of food to keep them occupied and they calmed right down.

Diane was feeling peckish herself. She realized that all she had eaten this morning was a box of chocolate biscuits and that hardly counted.

"I'm famished; I could do with a bite," she said as the cook began working on the sandwiches for the guests.

"What will you have? I've got chicken, roast beef or cucumber."

"The chicken sounds quite good," Diane answered.

Mrs. Allan handed her a cold chicken sandwich and a cup of tea. "You can stay right here and eat if you like. I wouldn't want to be out there, there is a killer staying in this hotel, can you believe it? Tea with a murderer is not my idea of good company. I would think stress like that would be bad for the digestion."

"Thank you, I think I will do just that." Diane sat down at a large round table and enjoyed her first real meal of the day.

"You write all those books about murders. What do you think? I think any one of the guests could be the perpetrator. I hope the MacKays learn their lesson and are much more particular about their guests in the future."

"I'm still waiting to see what the police have to say. It may be accidental."

"Not likely. Not with as many police as they have here. A detective came all the way from Inverness! Can you imagine?'

"Yes, I can." Diane finished the sandwich and tea. She was always able to think better when she had something in her stomach.

"You are welcome to stay in here with me where it's safe. I've got knives," said the cook cheerfully as she held up a large butcher's knife and smiled.

Diane nodded her head and realized that she preferred her chances in the great hall with the anxious guests and possibly a killer.

Diane returned to the great hall and walked up to the police officer guarding the staircase.

"Any chance I may be able to go up?"

"I'm afraid not."

"Right," said Diane as she turned and walked away.

She sat on the couch and took her phone out of her pocket. She pressed the power button and punched in her passcode, then texted Juliana.

Hope you don't mind, tea for the guests and refunds.

Juliana responded: *Tea ok. Refunds?*

Jk re refunds. Await rescue

Lol on my way

Diane turned her phone off and put it back in her pocket. She looked at the stairs and was pleased to see Juliana speaking with the police officer who was in charge of all entry to the second floor. After a few minutes' conversation, Juliana beckoned her to join her.

"May I go up?" asked Diane.

"Yes Inspector, I meant no disrespect."

"Just doing your duty, keep up the good work."

When Diane and Juliana reached the second-floor landing, Diane stopped the younger woman and in a whisper asked, "Inspector?"

"Yes, I told him that you are a retired Detective Inspector from Shropshire and that Inspector McNair requested your presence."

"Did he?"

"Of course not, but I'm certain he would if he knew you."

"Juliana, you are full of surprises. Remind me not to ever underestimate you."

The ladies walked down the second-floor corridor. Diane was certain that when Inspector McNair was confronted with a civilian trespassing in his crime scene, he was very likely to react less than cordially. She hoped to remain in the hall and just observe the investigation for now, and felt certain that she would have the opportunity to investigate the room where the body was found soon enough.

For now, she was just content to be out of the kitchen with the knife-wielding cook and away from the guests who were on the verge of anarchy. Besides, she reasoned observing a real police investigation was always a good source of material for her books. Juliana led Diane to the crime scene.

"I will just wait out here, I don't want to be in the way."

"I'm going to check in and see if the Inspector needs anything else."

"I will be right here."

Diane stood in the corridor and peered into Snelling's room. It was difficult to see very much from that angle, but she could tell from what she could see of the room that Juliana had been right; the room seemed to be in a state of disarray.

Juliana walked back out of Snelling's room looking white as a ghost.

"Juliana?"

"That room looks like a scene from a horror movie and Mr. Snelling is still there."

"Maybe you should go have a lie down."

"The Inspector needs a few more minor details from our reservation system and personnel files; after that, I may do just that."

Juliana walked back down the hall, leaving Diane on her own.

Diane stayed quiet and tried to blend into the scenery, as she knew that the gravity of the situation demanded it. Without her friends, the guests or the staff to offer her the faintest distraction, she was able to concentrate her thoughts on what little bit of information she knew.

A guest, Mr. James Snelling, had died in his room sometime last night. He had stayed at the hotel on a prior occasion. Malcolm had treated him for a heart condition. The room Mr. Snelling had been occupying and the room where he died looked as though it had been destroyed by a wild animal like a big cat. The paintings and walls had evidence of scratch marks. The deceased did not seem to have died as the result of an outside source, but of fright. Despite the room being destroyed, no one heard a sound, and there were no witnesses.

This was definitely a mystery. Diane played several scenarios in her mind and found that at this early stage in the investigation she had far more questions than she had definitive answers. At least, that was the case at the moment.

As she stood in the corridor waiting for the police to finish, she thought about what would have prompted someone to go through so much trouble to scare Mr. Snelling to death. She also pondered about the wild animal theory. She was unable to recall a single incident of a big cat or wild animal taking the time to attack the room of a man with a heart condition at a hotel. It was unprecedented.

"Have forensics get back to me with that report immediately. If they can't find the answer, have them contact a zoologist."

Diane watched a handsome, older gentleman leave Snelling's room. He was slightly younger with dark hair that was giving way to gray. He had piercing blue eyes and was easily six feet tall. She thought the Inspector was going to walk past her, but then he stopped in front of her. He looked at her as though he recognized her.

"I know you from somewhere, now let me see if I can place where that somewhere is," he said, his English spoken with a slight Inverness accent. He stared at her as though trying to decipher a difficult puzzle. Finally, he nodded his head and replied, "You're that mystery writer, from that village that sounds like a dessert, let see me... Apple something, that's right, Apple Mews."

"I am that mystery writer from Apple Mews; my name is Diane Dimbleby."

"I am Detective Inspector Robert McNair from Inverness."

"I do have a confession, Inspector, your officer at the staircase may be under the misguided impression that I am a retired Inspector."

"I'm sure there is a perfectly rational explanation for your criminal impersonation of a police officer," he said.

"A retired Inspector. I'm sure the penalty is not as strict."

"Alright Inspector, what brings you here? The thrill of murder? I have read some of your books, and they are quite good. You must have a dark side to write murder mysteries that are as convincing as you seem to do. I would say you have a real understanding of the criminal mind. What was your background, law enforcement?"

"No, actually this is my holiday, or at least it was supposed to be. A bit of birdwatching, some hiking and hours of good conversation with my friends that own this hotel. My background is education; I am a retired school teacher. I have found that nothing is quite as devious as an eight-year-old child with an agenda."

"Forgive me, I didn't it mean to be rude. The stress of this job can sometimes get to even the strongest of us," he apologized.

"Inspector, you are under a lot of stress, I understand. From what I can tell, this is not a cut and dried case, it's complicated."

"Thank you, I am glad you are here. I normally don't admit this to anyone, but I could use all the help I can get on this one. Would you terribly mind coming and having a look at the room? I must warn you though, Mr. Snelling, the occupant, is still in there."

"Inspector, I would be delighted to help out in any way that I can. You can count on my assistance."

"Thank you Inspector," he said with a wink that she found charming.

Inspector McNair returned to the room with Diane. Diane thought she had a good picture of what she would find once she entered the crime scene. She soon discovered that it was far worse than anything she could have imagined. Diane always prided herself on her ability to handle nearly any twisted machination the human mind could devise as a method of murder, but this scene was unlike anything she had ever witnessed.

Mr. Snelling was still in the room, as Inspector McNair had warned. That was always a sobering sight, she thought to herself. She looked at Snelling for any signs of what may have caused his untimely demise. This was grim work; he seemed to have died of fright. His face was still contorted in fear. From what she could tell, he did not have a scratch, bruise, or abrasion anywhere on his body that she could see from observation.

"Inspector, this may seem to be a premature question in light of the fact that the victim is still in here with us, but has your team managed to establish a cause of death?'

"We still need to do the lab work and autopsy, but right now, judging from the appearance of the body, no marks, or scratches, and the facial expression, I am working on the assumption that he died of a heart attack. His medical records would suggest a prior heart condition."

After studying Snelling, she examined the room for any details or clues that might stand out. In this case, the entire room stood out as a clue. She tried hard to suppress her reaction, which was to ask for a strong drink and walk away. The room was in a shambles and she found herself trying to imagine what manner of animal or human had terrorized Mr. Snelling in his final moments.

There were scratches on the walls that seemed to have been made by a creature with long claws or a madman. The paintings were all destroyed and smashed. Lamps, vases, or any decorative ornaments lay in pieces. She shuddered involuntarily as she tried to imagine Mr. Snelling in the room with whatever or whoever had been capable of the ferocity of this attack.

She noticed that the window to the room was covered in blood from the outside. She thought that was a curious detail.

"The blood on the outside of this window, has your team been able to determine if it's animal or human in origin?"

"At this stage, we believe that it's an animal, perhaps a bird."

"On the handle of the window or the glass, did you find any fingerprints?"

"We examined the glass and the handle and only discovered the fingerprints of Mr. Snelling."

Diane noticed that the window was shut now. She looked at the blood and thought that perhaps there may be a different explanation than the bird theory, but she did not yet have enough information to pose a conflicting theory. Diane decided that she would keep her ideas about the window to herself for now.

She retraced her steps now that the initial shock was wearing off. Entering a crime scene was often like jumping into a swimming pool; when you first get in the water is freezing, but after a while, you become acclimated to it. Now that she was becoming acclimated, she knew that she would be able to spot clues she may have missed in her preliminary search.

The room that Snelling had booked was quite large. It had been beautifully decorated and would have been an ideal place for a relaxing, romantic holiday. The paintings that were destroyed had been chosen with care, and the décor was evocative of an earlier, gracious time. She walked over to a painting that lay smashed on the floor. She looked at the picture and was surprised to see minuscule drops of blood on it.

"Inspector, what did you make of this?"

"Make of what? I don't believe my team found anything significant in that part of the room."

"These drops of blood; do you suppose they are from the same animal that rammed into the window?"

"Drops of blood?"

The Inspector strode across the room and joined her at the painting. He crouched down beside her and peered at the drops of the blood on the picture.

"It would seem that forensics missed those, darn sloppy work. I will get someone over here to take samples right away."

The Inspector walked away and, from the sounds of the conversation, he was not pleased. A forensics investigator soon joined Diane at the picture and collected the sample.

"What have you found about the guests? Anything that would suggest a motive or a connection?" she asked as she joined him by the fireplace.

He looked up from his cell phone and answered, "The guests appear for the most part to have clean records. There is one guest, a Simon Berry, who I may want to investigate further. He has a record, and it may be circumstantial, but it does make him a person of interest in this investigation."

"He has a record? What type of record?"

"He was arrested for communicating threats to destroy a research facility that conducted experiments on animals. He threatened to blow it up."

"Hmm. That is interesting, and the other guests, are they free to leave?"

"Not yet. This case is not your run-of-the-mill shooting or stabbing. This is something far more diabolical. I am afraid that whoever is responsible for Mr. Snelling's death went through considerable pains to execute this elaborate murder. And judging from the state of this scene, he or she must be considered to be dangerous, and I would dare say capable of anything."

Diane was not normally quick to jump to conclusions. She was practical and steady in her thinking and not prone to panic. She looked around the room with the claw marks on the walls and the blood on the window. She thought about the guests downstairs and wondered which one may be capable of such violence. She decided that maybe Mrs. Allan in the kitchen with her butcher knife was not as paranoid as she seemed.

Chapter 3

It was late in the afternoon when Snelling's body was carried out of the hotel. Juliana and Malcolm had taken care to ensure that the guests were in the library and did not have to witness such a sobering sight. Inspector McNair and his team were not far behind. It had been a long day, and the investigation was just getting underway.

Snelling's room remained closed, and the guests were not allowed to leave the premises, but they were allowed to return to their rooms. Police officers remained at the hotel to protect the guests and to ensure that no one left yet. The Inspector was hoping to clear this matter up as soon as possible. In the meantime, all the guests and the staff were ordered to stay put.

The stress of the day and the current situation was a bit much for everyone and tensions were high. Malcolm invited the guests to the hotel lounge for complimentary drinks after dinner. Diane took him up on his invitation, as did nearly everyone else. The lounge reminded her of the pub in Apple Mews. It was a large room that looked out over a view of the ocean. Dark wood and red leather furniture gave the pub a cozy ambiance.

Diane sat at a table with Juliana and Malcolm. She was indulging in a pint and so was Malcolm, while Juliana only stared at her glass of wine. They had all had a terrible day, but no one worse than Snelling. Diane could not get the crime scene out of her mind. She was certain that her companions were still as horrified by the events of the last several hours as she was.

She could not help but notice that her companions looked at the hotel guests warily as they sipped their drinks. They had good reason considering what Diane knew about the facts of the case. She pondered all the possibilities and every scenario she could imagine. Mr. Snelling was found dead in a room that had been destroyed violently by someone or something. He did not have a scratch on him, and no one had heard anything.

She just could not picture a scenario in which an animal or bird would enter a hotel room and smash everything to bits. Judging from the blood that was in the room, she wondered why anything would attack paintings and decorative objects so violently, or scratch the walls and not touch the victim.

She knew she was missing something. If she could only find that piece of evidence, she was certain that she would be able to put all the pieces together just like a puzzle and they would all fit perfectly. Right now, all she had was two corners and a handful of pieces that didn't match. She sipped her drink and considered asking for something a little stronger.

"Malcolm, I don't know anything about Mr. Snelling. Can you tell me why you think anyone would want to murder him and in such a dramatic fashion? Poor soul."

"He was the local veterinarian, but that's not all," he answered as he lowered his voice.

Juliana and Diane leaned in to listen as Malcolm continued, "He stayed at the hotel and met a friend, a lady friend from Inverness. I can't be certain, but I believe she was married."

"That might be an important fact. A love triangle, how interesting," whispered Diane.

She looked around the lounge at the other guests and caught the eye of Simon Berry. Diane was left with the distinct impression that he had been trying to listen to their conversation. His hasty departure soon afterward confirmed her suspicion.

"Our victim was involved in a possible love triangle and ends up dead at the hotel he stayed at with his paramour, that is a place to start. Can you think of anything unusual or out of the ordinary that happened in the last few days?"

"Juliana, would you say what happened with Jeffery was unusual?" asked Malcolm.

"Yes, I suppose, I would. I had not considered it until now," answered Juliana.

"Jeffery?" asked Diane as she looked around the lounge.

"Diane, you remember our hotel parrot, we call her Jeffery," Malcolm asked.

"Oh yes, the parrot, now what about him?"

"He is a girl, but that's a long story. Jeffery had her cage stolen two days ago. I'm sure you can understand our shock when we discovered her flying around the hotel," said Malcolm

"We could not imagine who would do something so odd. We went out and bought her a brand-new cage. Here's the part you are sure to love; her cage turned up this morning right after Mr. Snelling was murdered," replied Juliana.

"That is unusual. I would say that certainly qualifies."

Diane had one more pint with Juliana and Malcolm before retiring for the evening. She needed time to think about the case logically. She took a shower and changed into her comfiest clothes, then unpacked her laptop and set it on the antique writing desk. She plugged it into the socket on the wall and powered it up.

She kept thinking about animals and birds and was having difficulty explaining how any creature ended up in the bedroom with Snelling. She stared at the empty search bar for several minutes before she realized that an animal or bird would have to have been lured into the room. She typed the words *How animals are lured* into the search bar and read several articles on the subject. She researched websites and read reports by experts. She found that they all shared a technique in common: noise. Noise was the main method to lure animals.

Diane researched the subject until she could no longer hold her eyes open. She was exhausted and needed rest. She powered off the laptop, then checked to be sure her door and window were both locked securely before climbing under the covers of the exquisitely carved four-poster bed.

As she switched off her bedside lamp, she thought about the articles she read and the clue she may have uncovered. If animals were lured by noise, then she knew what she needed to do. Tomorrow would be a busy and with any luck, productive day. Even with the knowledge that there was a killer on the loose, she snuggled under the covers and soon fell asleep.

Chapter 4

The next morning, Diane was out of bed at an early hour. She dressed quickly and rushed downstairs to get a quick bite and a cup of tea. She needed fuel for the day ahead, so she turned to her old favorite, a Scottish breakfast. She sat down to a breakfast plate loaded with sausage, black pudding, egg, mushrooms, and tomatoes. She enjoyed fresh marmalade with toast and a good strong cup of tea.

After breakfast, she was ready to start the investigation, and she knew just where she needed to look: the lost and found. Diane went to the study and knocked on the door.

"Come in." She heard Juliana's voice from behind the door.

"Mind if I make a small request?"

"No, Diane you are family to us, what would you like?" asked Juliana as she looked up from her laptop.

"I was wondering if I might take a quick peek at your lost and found?"

"The lost and found? I'm afraid there hasn't been anything interesting in there for months, but you are welcome to it."

"Thank you," said Diane. Juliana led her to the office where the cupboard marked lost and found was located. "You are welcome to use the desk, let me know if you need anything," said Juliana as she closed the door.

Diane searched through the cupboard and found the usual items one might expect to reside in a hotel lost and found. She found keys of every shape and description, caps, hats, umbrellas, and a box of lighters. Juliana was right, there really wasn't much to it, at least nothing interesting.

Diane sat at the desk and thought about what her next move should be. She had examined the lost and found and discovered nothing. Now, she needed to do something a little more drastic. She thought about how she wanted to word her next request and try as she might, was unable to find a way to make the next request not sound a little mad. She decided that if solving this case required her to exhibit a touch of madness, then she was willing to accept that.

She left the office and returned to the study. Diane hesitated before she knocked on the door. She knew that this request was going to be met with resistance and she steeled herself for it. She strengthened her resolve and knocked.

"Come in," said Juliana.

"I don't mean to be a pest, but I have another request."

"Diane, anything you ask is yours." Juliana said as she continued typing on her laptop.

"I was wondering if you might loan me every available staff member you have to go through the hotel rubbish?"

"What?" asked Juliana as she stopped typing and looked at Diane as if trying to comprehend the words she had said and was unable to make rational sense of them.

"The rubbish and your staff. I need every available person to assist me. I'm quite aware that this sounds mad. I assure you, it's for the investigation."

"Diane, there must be some other way, please say that there is."

"I am afraid not, there is a bright side to this. If I find what I think may be hiding in the rubbish, then the killer can be caught. You will be able to return to business as usual without worrying that you have rented a room to a dangerous, violent criminal."

"Well put. I will call the staff."

A half hour later, Diane and Juliana met with every available member of housekeeping, cooking and hospitality outside at the hotel rubbish container. No one looked enthused to be there. No one, except Diane, who seemed to be quite cheerful despite the nasty looks she was getting from several members of the staff, particularly the kitchen employees.

"Staff," began Juliana, "I have assembled you here to ask for your assistance. This may seem unpleasant, but I am certain that if we all pull together as a team; I feel confident that the investigation can be concluded quickly. Now if you will give your attention to Mrs. Dimbleby."

"I am confident that no one wants to go through the rubbish, least of all me," said Diane.

"I'd say you're right about that," said a young man standing in the back of the crowd,

"Do we have to?" asked a maid.

"I understand, I do, but I am sure that none of you enjoy being trapped at the hotel and told you can't leave by the police," Diane stated.

Many of the staff nodded their heads in agreement.

"If we are successful in our search today, I can assure that it will speed up the investigation and help the police find the killer. If you will assist me in going through all the rubbish in this container and in every room, including staff offices, that would be greatly appreciated."

"How appreciated, like a bonus or a raise?" asked the young man from the back. The staff laughed at his remark and then, resigned to their fate, walked towards the gigantic container.

"Just what exactly are we supposed to be looking for, anyway?" asked a valet with a scowl.

"Preferably a whistle or anything that makes noise or stands out as being unusual."

"Staff, I have gloves, line up and get a pair of gloves," said Juliana as she looked over at Diane and whispered, "I sure hope you know what you're doing, I may lose some of my staff after this."

"Juliana, I have a theory and if it's right, we might be able to find out what happened to Mr. Snelling. That has got to be worth losing a few disgruntled employees."

"It's not the disgruntled ones I care about, they would not leave if you begged them, it's the good ones I have to consider."

Juliana had a good point, and Diane felt terrible about asking Juliana's staff to dig through the rubbish. She knew that it was not part of the staff's job descriptions, but she also knew with a hotel of this size there was simply no other way to have completed this job alone. Well, there was, but it might have taken days, and by then the killer could have struck again or escaped.

Diane put on a pair of kitchen gloves and dug into the bags of rubbish. The staff were still grumbling but at least they were working, thought Diane as she opened bag after bag of garbage. She didn't discover anything but snack wrappers, drink cans and tissue. She walked around to see if anyone else was having any luck, but all anyone could find was rubbish.

An hour later, Diane was beginning to wonder if this was an exercise in futility. The staff were grumbling even more, and so far, no one had found anything useful. Although, they had found some interesting rubbish from one of the guest rooms that made several female staff members and even a few of the males blush.

"Diane, I don't think we are going to find what you are looking for," said Juliana.

"Just a little longer, I know there has to be something here," Diane said as she returned her attention to a bag of rubbish.

"Is this it?" asked a young woman from the kitchen staff.

"Let's see, what have you got there?" asked Diane.

The young woman handed her a whistle. Diane was overjoyed. "Yes, this is it! Well done everyone," she said cheerfully.

She looked at the whistle and wiped it on her pants. It had been in the trash and who knows who had their lips on it, but she wanted to see what would happen. She blew it expecting to hear a high-pitched sound, but there was silence instead.

"That might be why they threw it away; that whistle is broke," joked an employee as several staff members joined him in laughter.

"If everyone would help to clean up, I believe we are finished here," said Juliana to her staff.

"Thank you for all of your assistance," said Diane as she examined the whistle. There was no detail about it that stood out to her, so she tried to illicit a response. Diane walked around the hotel grounds with the whistle and blew it; still there was no sound and more importantly no reaction by anything or anyone. She did this several times before returning to her room.

She put the whistle down on the desk beside the laptop. After the search through the lost and found and then the rubbish, she decided that she needed a few minutes to let her mind rest. She switched on the TV. She searched the channels looking for anything interesting and found one of her favorite shows, "Cash in the Attic."

Diane sat down on the coach and was just getting comfortable when she realized something very important that she had overlooked. She turned off the TV, then put the whistle in her pocket along with her room key. She wasn't sure whether Juliana would be as accommodating to any more requests as she was earlier, not after the search through the rubbish, but Diane knew this one was worth a try.

She rushed downstairs and returned to the study. She knocked.

"Come in," said Juliana.

"Oh God, not the rubbish again," said Juliana.

"No, not the rubbish again. This time, I was wondering if I might have a peek at your attic?"

"I have no idea what could possibly be of any interest in the attic, but why not? Follow me, and you are going to need this." Juliana handed her a torch from the first aid supplies on the shelf by the door.

Juliana led Diana up the staircase and down a hall and up another set of stairs, down one more corridor and finally up a narrow, dark set of old creaky wooden stairs to a door. Juliana opened the door and Diane turned on the torch.

"Be careful, I'm not sure how good the floor is up here."

"Thank you. Don't worry about me, I'll be fine."

Juliana went back downstairs and left Diane to her investigation. Diane walked into the attic and was surprised by how utterly dark it was. It reminded her of classic horrors movies and ghost stories. She tried not to think about that, not with a real-life killer roaming around.

She shined the torch in all directions looking for anything that might be important. The attic was empty except for a small scrap of tartan cloth she found on a nail. She turned the torch's light to the material and observed that it was torn. Its pattern was thin, white horizontal and vertical lines with thick, black horizontal and vertical lines on a red background. She carefully put the torn piece of tartan in her pocket.

As she continued her search, she noticed a faint, fluttering sound. Diane listened carefully, trying to detect what could have made that sound when she had a moment of clarity. She pulled the whistle from her pocket and blew it. She expected a reaction, but was only met with silence. She thought about it and then decided to blow the whistle several times. Although she could not hear the sound of the whistle, something in the darkness heard it and reacted to it.

She heard the unmistakable sound of fluttering, lots of fluttering. She shined the torch above her head and saw a cloud of bats flying overhead in the eaves of the old attic. Suddenly, a bat swooped in and sailed right past her head.

She assessed her situation and decided that maybe it was best all-around if she called it a day. She shined the torch upward, illuminating the bats once more, then quietly walked to the attic door. She closed the attic door softly and turned off the torch, then made her way down the creaky stairs and to the corridor towards her room.

Chapter 5

Diane sat back in the wicker chair and gazed at a delightful view. It was a beautiful summer's day; the sky was a brilliant blue with fluffy white clouds. Sunlight danced on the waves of the sea. From her seat on the terrace, the view was peaceful and serene. Inside the hotel, all was not peaceful nor serene.

The staff were still grumbling about the rubbish search yesterday, the guests were losing patience with the police and Juliana and Malcolm, and the kitchen staff were planning a mutiny unless they were allowed to go home. A valet and a maid had tried to escape last night, but they were quickly returned to the hotel. Meanwhile, there was still a dangerously unhinged killer on the loose, or perhaps a wild, vicious animal. The result was a palpable tension. Diane was convinced that unless this case was solved soon, the situation might escalate into anarchy.

She looked at the view and waited patiently for her lunch to arrive. She always enjoyed having lunch outside on the hotel terrace when she stayed at the Glen Gorm Hotel. The incredible view and the delicious food were always a relaxing combination. She noticed that her food order seemed to be taking longer than normal, which she assumed was retaliation for the rubbish search.

Diane realized she needed to solve this case before total chaos gripped the hotel. To a casual observer, it may appear that she was relaxing and on holiday, but nothing could be farther from the truth. The view and the fresh air were a potent drug; they were vital to the clear, analytical thinking that she needed to solve this case.

Yesterday had been very productive. She thought about the new clues that had come to light. She watched the seagulls flying above the water and considered how the clues fit together. She also wondered about the mysterious woman that Malcolm had mentioned. Who was this woman that was having an affair with Mr. Snelling? Could this be a motive?

Diane was so deep in thought that she did not notice that Inspector McNair had joined her until he greeted her.

"Mrs. Dimbleby, if I may have a word?"

"Inspector McNair, if you would like to join me for lunch, I believe I can accommodate your request," Diane answered warmly. Inspector McNair had dark circles under his eyes from lack of rest. Diane concluded that he was the type of detective that did not sleep until a case was solved.

"If I will not be intruding, I would love to accept your offer. I am famished," Inspector McNair admitted as he sat down in a wicker chair at Diane's table.

"I am not surprised. With a case as pressing as this one, I would not hesitate to say that you are not eating or sleeping very much."

"You are correct in your assessment. It sounds like you understand this line of work very well."

"My late husband was a detective at Scotland Yard."

"The Yard, that is impressive. I bet you do know a thing or two about the messy ones, the cases that grip you until you solve them or you go mad in the attempt."

"Yes, Inspector McNair, I do, and this case seems to be messy indeed."

"I find it exasperating when the murderer gets creative. If only they would stick to the tried-and-true methods such as shooting or stabbing. With the right forensics team and a solid motive, those cases can be solved without much fuss, unlike this one."

"Inspector, I am glad that you are joining me for lunch, although I should warn you that service may be less than stellar today. I seem to have made enemies of the kitchen staff."

"Would it be worth it for me to inquire how that may have happened?"

"I am afraid that is a story best left for after the investigation is concluded."

A surly waitress arrived at the table with Diane's lunch order. The soup smelled delicious, and the sandwich was piled high with roast beef. The Inspector did not need a menu; he ordered the soup and sandwich as well. The waitress did not say a word as she took down his order and left the table in a huff.

"I would recommend having your food tested for toxic or poisonous substances," Inspector McNair said with a smile.

"The cook may be a bit eccentric, but the food here is quite good. I am willing to take the chance," Diane answered cheerfully, then switched gears, "You are obviously not here for lunch."

"No, I am afraid not. I am still in the thick of this investigation, I was hoping that we might be able to compare notes. I am sure that a writer of murder mysteries has not been sitting idly by watching television in the middle of an active homicide investigation."

"Detective, you are quite right, I have not been sitting idle at all. What do you know about Mr. Snelling and his romantic life? Was he having an affair with a married woman?"

"He was the local veterinarian, and he came to the hotel to meet his lover, a Mrs. Katie Munro. Mrs. Munro is married, but separated from her husband, a Mr. Thomas Munro."

The waitress returned with the Inspector's order. He dug into the sandwich as though he had never seen food before.

"Inspector, was Mr. Munro aware that his wife was having an affair?"

"Yes, he knew about it. Although he knew that his wife was involved in an adulterous relationship, he still lived with her. They maintained the façade of being married even though they were in the middle of divorce proceedings. The couple's separation and divorce were kept secret. Their family and friends were unaware they were even having marital issues."

Diane thought about Mrs. Munro. What must the woman of Mr. Snelling's dreams be like? She concluded that this woman must be extraordinary to inspire someone, perhaps her husband, to commit murder. If so, the obvious suspect, the jealous husband, was really a suspect.

"Do you consider Mr. Munro to be a suspect?"

"It is too early in the investigation to name suspects. At this stage, I would say that I am open to nearly any possibility, although I do have to admit, Mr. Munro does have a solid motive," admitted the Inspector as he took another bite of sandwich. "Thomas and his wife came down together for a wedding across the water in Mallaig. I'm sure he must have known that his wife's lover lived in Skye and was in fact staying at the hotel also, but Mr. Munro denies knowing that."

"Is it possible that as ghastly as the crime scene appeared and the existence of a love triangle, that this is not a murder? Do you think that Mr. Snelling may be the victim of death by misadventure?"

"You do bring up a good point. I have considered that as a possibility. However, at this stage, I must investigate his death as a probable murder. His affair with Mrs. Munro would be a strong motive. It is true that Mr. Snelling died of fright, but what was he so afraid of and what viciously attacked the room, but not the victim?"

"Inspector, I think I may have a theory that may answer the question of what attacked Mr. Snelling. I believe it may be bats."

"Bats? What gives you the impression that it was bats?"

"I conducted a little research and discovered that animals can be lured or summoned by sound. A whistle was discovered in the rubbish yesterday. This whistle cannot be heard by humans, but can be heard by bats."

"Are you quite sure that it was not a whistle for training dogs or other animals?"

"I conducted my own unofficial testing. The only creatures that reacted to it were bats."

"Hmm, bats you say. I will consider that theory. I will have the lab test for the presence of bats at the crime scene. I am not sure that I want the details, but how did you manage to determine the whistle could only be heard by bats?"

"Inspector, I followed the not-so-strictly-logical investigation technique known as a bit of luck and an educated guess."

The unplanned lunch meeting with the Inspector gave Diane much to think about that evening. This murder was still an unsolved puzzle to put together. She felt as though she had acquired more of the pieces.

Now, if she could just fit them together, she might be able to get a better idea of what was missing. At the very minimum, it would give her a place to start, because right now she was frustrated.

Without a new breakthrough or clue, her investigation was at a standstill. Right now, she had a few solid clues, but there just wasn't enough to arrive at a logical explanation. It was maddening. She decided that the best course of action was to try to get some rest and start fresh tomorrow. A good night's sleep was necessary for optimal cognitive functioning and this case required nothing less than optimal.

The following morning after breakfast, she decided that a change of focus might be just the thing to calm her nerves and sharpen her concentration skills. She returned to her room, sat down at her desk and powered on her laptop. She had enjoyed a good night's sleep and now decided to focus her energy on her writing. Writing had always calmed her nerves and improved her ability to concentrate. She opened the file containing her book and started typing.

Chapter 6

Diane wrote for many hours that day and decided to reward herself after dinner with a pint in the lounge. She sat at a table, enjoying a sip of her reward when she saw Inspector McNair enter the lounge. He walked directly to her table.

"Are you still on duty?" Diane asked.

"Yes, I am. I consider myself always on duty during a case. Although, to tell you the truth, I do intend on having a drink the moment I have successfully apprehended a suspect."

"Won't you please join me?' she asked graciously, offering to share her table.

"You are probably convinced that I am stalking you," he joked.

"It would seem that way. Can I buy a round of your nonalcoholic beverage of choice?"

"Thank you, no, but I hope you allow me to buy you a drink. Your assistance has proven to be invaluable."

"I am glad to hear that I was able to be helpful. I just wanted to do my bit."

Inspector McNair looked at the other guests in the lounge and lowered his voice. "You were right about the bats. The lab tested the droplets of blood on the carpet and discovered that it tested positive for being bat in origin. Excellent work, Inspector Dimbleby."

"Bats. Was it a single animal or several?"

"From the evidence that we have gathered at this stage, it would appear that there were several animals involved in the attack. The amount of damage and the severity of it support that theory. The blood found on the window also tested positive for bat. We are now actively searching for the injured animal."

Diane had experienced a few minor twinges of guilt when she asked the hotel staff to dig through the rubbish. Discovering that the police could confirm her suspicions based on the evidence obtained in that search, now made all the delayed lunches and surly staff attitudes worth it. The staff may still be angry about being put on rubbish detail, but when the case was solved and the killer was arrested, their hard work would have made it possible.

"Now that we have the who solved thanks to your brilliant insight, what about the sound problem?" asked McNair "How was it possible that no one heard a single sound? A violent attack by several bats and a man screaming should have attracted the attention of the guests staying in the nearby rooms. I just don't understand how no one heard a sound."

"That problem bothered me as well. A man is alone in his room, and flying mammals suddenly attack him. It is enough to give anyone nightmares. I agree he would have been screaming as the bats attacked and destroyed his room. Considering the level of destruction present in that room, it could not have been anything less than chaos. Bats were breaking lamps and destroying paintings. It must have been quite a commotion."

"Exactly. A man is screaming, lamps breaking and paintings being smashed. This incident generated enough noise to have woken up, at the very minimum, his next-door neighbors. The question remains, how did this terrible scene play out without anyone so much as hearing a cry for help?"

Diane thought about that question and took a deep breath. She was lost in concentration as she stared at a painting on the wall across from her. It was a painting of the Glen Gorm Hotel. The picture showed the Glen Gorm Hotel at sunset overlooking the sea like a mighty castle or fortress.

She stared at the painting pondering the question of the noise that no one heard when a thought suddenly occurred to her. The Glen Gorm Hotel was an old medieval castle. She looked from the picture to the walls of the lounge, and the solution came to her in a flash.

The hotel was not built of brick; it had been constructed of large blocks of stone. She stood up as the Inspector watched her with a quizzical look on his face. She walked to the wall and examined the stone. She returned to her seat at the table with an answer.

"This hotel was not built to resemble a castle, Inspector. It actually is an old castle."

"My dear Mrs. Dimbleby, what does the construction of the hotel mean to this investigation?"

"The walls were built of heavy, thick stone. If the window and door was closed to his room, no one would have heard a sound. I would hazard to guess that you could fire a gun in Mr. Snelling's room and not one single person would have heard it because the thick walls are acting as a soundproof barrier."

The Inspector looked at Diane and tried to make sense of what she had just revealed. He also stood up and walked to the wall. He looked at the heavy stone blocks and thought about the stone walls in Snelling's room. He would have forensics test the theory, but he felt confident that they would discover that what Mrs. Dimbleby said was correct.

"I never would have concluded that the walls were acting as a soundproof barrier. Well done."

She was collecting more pieces of the puzzle. The blood on the floor and the window was bats, and the walls were soundproof, now what about a motive? Although Mr. Munro seems to have an obvious motive, was he the only possible suspect?

"I am sure you are aware of this, but with the clues you have in your possession, your next logical step would be to concentrate on a motive."

"You are right, if I can establish a strong motive then I will feel like I am on solid ground with this case. I may even get some rest and eat a meal," Inspector McNair said as he looked at Diane with a warm smile. "I do have Mr. Munro. He has a very strong motive but he also has an alibi."

"He has an alibi? Have you interviewed him?"

"Yes, I did. I have never been a man who displays his emotions. I suppose I am naïve in my assumption that most people I come across maintain that same standard, chalk it up to my time spent in the Royal Navy and lifelong police work. I pride myself on my calm demeanor, but Mr. Munro seems to be opposite in every way. It was glaringly obvious that he was the jealous type."

"Jealous? Do you believe he was jealous enough to commit murder?"

Inspector McNair recounted the details regarding Mr. Munro, "The husband is the quintessential jealous husband suspect. His jealous behavior has been observed by friends and probably even total strangers. He behaves poorly, and he knows about his wife's affair."

"You mentioned earlier that he has an alibi?"

"Yes, he and Katie both have an alibi that checks out. The night that Mr. Snelling was murdered, they were attending a wedding in Mallaig. The guests of the wedding reported seeing the couple."

"The ferry runs late during the summer between the Skye and Mallaig, perhaps they came back on the ferry during the wedding?"

His calm demeanor slipped just a bit into frustration when he answered, "The ferry crews working that night remember seeing Mr. and Mrs. Munro coming and going right on schedule for the wedding. I have checked the ferry timetable, and everything seems to check out with their story."

Diane quietly asked, "Where would they have been at the time of the murder?"

"They would have been on the mainland at the time of death. The ferry schedule for that night would not have made a return trip to the hotel and then back to Mallaig during the wedding possible."

"Let me be sure that I understand, Mr. Munro is involved in a secret divorce from his wife. He is incredibly jealous, and he knew about her affair with Mr. Snelling. He has the best motive for murder, and he has a strong alibi. What about Katie Munro? Have you interviewed her yet?"

"No, I have not, I have been concentrating on Mr. Munro because of his temperament and motive. Mr. Munro was a jealous husband, and Katie was the wife with the lover. Why would Katie have killed the man she was willing to risk everything for, especially her marriage? The husband knew about the affair, so it was too late to silence Mr. Snelling if he threatened to expose her. I just do not see a clear motive."

"Katie Munro may have a motive even stronger than her husband. A woman in love is capable of nearly anything."

"Precisely, if she was in love with Mr. Snelling, why would she have killed him? She was involved in a divorce that would soon free her to be with her lover."

"Inspector, let's assume for a moment that it was not Mr. Snelling that she was in love with. What if she truly loved her husband, that he was the love of her life? Consider that Mr. Snelling may only have been a fling or a casual affair."

"I believe I see where you are heading with this line of thinking; you are telling me that I need to look at it from a different perspective and consider that love is not the only reason women commit adultery. I believe that you are implying to stop being a caveman about my views on women."

"I am sure you are not a caveman, but it is a mistake that men find easy to make. They forget that women can be motivated by lust only without love. I imagine that she met James Snelling and the sparks flew. There was a certain something about him that she found irresistible, and they began an affair. I assume that she enjoyed their time together. It was romantic and exciting to have a secret lover."

"I understand that she may not have loved Snelling, but what would be her motivation to murder him in a violent manner?" asked Inspector McNair as he listened in rapt attention.

"In this scenario, she has enjoyed her time with Snelling; the sensual interludes, the romantic hotel and the novelty of a new love must have proven to be intoxicating. She may have felt torn between her love and loyalty for her husband and the lust that she felt with Snelling."

"In this scenario, you believe that it is possible that she felt torn between lust for her lover, Mr. Snelling, and the strong ties of love that she felt for her husband. If that was the case, then what is her motivation?"

"If Katie truly loved her husband, I believe that she would be capable of nearly anything to protect her relationship with the man she loved. She enjoyed the fun and thrill of a secret romance, but she was never willing to leave her husband or sacrifice her marriage for Snelling. Her husband found out about the affair, loses his temper and sues for divorce. This was a catastrophe for Katie. She may have felt forced to do whatever was necessary to protect her marriage."

"Once again, you have proven invaluable. You have given me a lot of good information. I will have the lab research the soundproof qualities of the stone used in the construction of this hotel. I believe that I will take your advice and arrange to interview Katie Munro."

The Inspector stood up and said, "I want to thank you for your assistance in this case. I look forward to taking you out to dinner to celebrate when this case is closed." Inspector McNair left the lounge and Diane was left alone with her thoughts.

Penelope Sotheby

Chapter 7

Diane sat in the lounge after the Inspector left. She was in possession of several new pieces of the puzzle; she just needed to put it together. She thought about all the likely scenarios that led to Mr. Snelling's death and realized that she was still not sure of the identity of the killer.

Mr. Munro seemed a likely culprit, but jealous husbands normally committed murder in fits of passion, not in a cold, calculated manner. Using bats in a soundproof room took real creativity and planning. She could not recall seeing a more bizarre set of circumstances in a murder case. She was convinced that she was unlikely to see anything to match it in the future.

She returned to her room, changed into her favorite pajamas and powered on the laptop. She opened the file containing her book and started typing. She knew that a good night's rest would help her see the case differently in the morning, but she was wide awake. Writing always helped her to focus, so she began working on her book.

As she worked on the novel, a small detail kept bothering her. Bats were used in the murder of Mr. Snelling. Bats were animals. Simon Berry, a guest of the hotel, was arrested for threatening to blow up a research facility that used animals for testing. Diane spun those facts around in her mind. It was possible that Simon had given up his violent ways to express his views, but to attack a local veterinarian with animals seemed bizarre and potentially motivated by something other than jealousy.

Diane stopped typing and stared at her laptop. Was Simon involved? This was conjecture at this stage, but it did warrant a bit more research. The blue glow of the laptop illuminated a woman in deep concentration. It may not prove to be anything, but Diane had a feeling, an instinct that there was something more to Simon and his decision to spend a few nights at the Glen Gorm Hotel.

She returned to typing and decided to tell Inspector McNair her thoughts about Simon when she spoke to him again. The words flowed easily as she worked on her novel for another hour before going to bed.

The next morning, Inspector McNair arrived at the hotel early. This investigation was far from over, and he wanted to make every minute of the day count. He wanted to get this case solved. He looked at his reflection in the rear-view mirror. The dark circles under his eyes were getting darker and more pronounced every day. His reflection revealed the exhaustion he felt. He hoped to solve this case soon; he needed the rest.

Up until last night, he thought he was through with the Munros and could cross them off his list of potential suspects. Mr. Munro was jealous and had demonstrated his lack of discretion regarding his displays of emotion, but he had not considered Katie Munro to have a motive for murder, until now. Last night at the lounge, Diane Dimbleby presented him with a convincing argument that proved there might be more to Katie Munro than he previously thought.

The hotel manager greeted him at the front desk with a less-than-cheerful salutation. This case was dragging on, and he needed to wrap it up so that he could allow the guests and staff to leave the hotel. The manager called the Munros' room and spoke with Katie. Katie would be right down, she told the Inspector.

"I need to speak with Mrs. Munro privately, is there an office available?"

"You can use my office, Inspector, I hope you let us go home soon."

"That makes two of us," he answered.

Katie Munro did not keep him waiting at the front desk for long. Looking at this petite woman, he was unsure that she would be capable of the cold-blooded cruelty required to murder Mr. Snelling. She was dressed in jeans and a t-shirt, her light brown hair was pulled back in a ponytail, and she spoke in a soft, gentle voice. Mrs. Dimbleby convinced him to speak with Katie, but he was far from convinced that this woman could harm anyone or anything.

"Mrs. Munro, I am terribly sorry to disturb you early in the morning. I hope you don't mind. I just have a few questions."

"Inspector, I don't mind in the least. I am happy to help any way that I can, although I'm not sure I can tell you anything useful," she said in a voice barely above a whisper.

He looked at Katie and tried to be objective. He had been a detective for many years, and he knew that he did not have to ask a lot of questions to uncover the information that he needed from a suspect; he just needed to ask the right questions. Snelling's killer had lured bats into his room and used them as a weapon. He wondered if this soft-spoken, demure woman had any knowledge of animal behavior that may prove interesting.

"I do not mean to be insensitive, but I need to know a few details about your relationship with Mr. Snelling. You may start by telling me how you met."

The expression on Katie's face changed, and she looked as though she might begin to cry. "This is very hard for me, Inspector, I hope you understand, I still can't believe that he is dead."

"Take your time, Mrs. Munro."

"I met James at Westhill, it's the lab that I work at in Inverness. We conducted experiments on animal behavior. I am not sure how it all started. I enjoyed working with him. It was a nice change to have someone that I could talk to about my work that really understood it, that was genuinely interested in the research I was conducting. He was so attentive to me, even in the lab. He was romantic and attentive, not like my husband."

Inspector McNair was struck by what Katie said, not about her relationship but about her line of work. He was disappointed in himself. How could he have been so careless as to overlook a vital detail that could be important to the case?

"Your research that you conducted in animal behavior, what animals did you use for your experiments?"

"Squirrels, mostly."

"Squirrels, that must have been fascinating and lively research," he said with a warm smile.

"Yes, it is. Squirrels are very energetic." Katie answered, brightly. She no longer appeared to be on the verge of tears. She looked at the Inspector and seemed to relax as she laughed about the squirrels.

"Tell me, Mrs. Munro, did you conduct research with any other animals, such as bats?" he asked.

Katie no longer looked relaxed. Her demeanor changed as she repeated the word, "Bats?"

"Yes, bats, did you and Mr. Snelling conduct research on bats and their behavior?"

"Yes Inspector, we did."

"How interesting. I appreciate your time this morning, I will be in touch if I have any more questions," he said as he stood up and walked to the front of the desk.

Katie stood to leave, "I hope you find whoever is responsible, this has all been so terrible."

"Yes, it has. Thank you, Mrs. Munro."

Returning to the front desk, he requested the manager ring Mrs. Dimbleby's room. She rolled her eyes and called Diane's room. There was no answer. He needed to see Diane before he left the hotel. He thanked the manager and looked at his watch. It was 8:30 in the morning. Perhaps she was having breakfast, he reasoned.

His hunch proved to be correct; he found Diane in the cheerful, sunny breakfast room. She had just sat down to enjoy a cup of tea and full Scottish breakfast when she saw the Inspector.

"Inspector, good morning, care to join me?"

"As much as I would love to say yes, I am in a hurry. I need to speak with you."

"Yes, of course."

The Inspector pulled up a chair beside her, "I hope you don't mind the close quarters, but I don't want to be overheard."

"You are quite alright, Inspector, what did you want to tell me?"

"You were right to suspect Katie. I interviewed her this morning and made an interesting discovery. I need to investigate further, but I may be close to making a real breakthrough."

Diane was overcome with curiosity. "What did you discover?"

"Mr. Snelling and Katie were more than lovers, they were coworkers. They worked together at a research facility that conducted research on animal behavior."

"That is interesting, it can't be a coincidence."

"I don't think it is either, I just need to investigate this lead and see where it goes."

"What type of animals did she and Mr. Snelling work with?'

"Squirrels, and prepare yourself for this, bats."

"Bats? Inspector, I would have to say you may be onto something. Where are you off to in such a hurry?"

"I am going back to Inverness. I want to check out the lab, ask a few questions."

Diane thought about Simon, the bats, and his criminal record. She suggested to the Inspector, "If you are going to ask questions at the lab, I would find out if they had received any threats recently."

"That's not a bad idea, I will be sure to check into that. I have got to get going, I'll talk to you soon."

Chapter 8

It was after lunch when Inspector McNair arrived at the Westhill Research Laboratory in Inverness. Trees shaded the parking of the modern glass and metal building. He selected a parking place for visitors in the shaded part of the lot and walked to the entrance. He opened the door and was blasted with a wave of cool air. It felt good after the long drive. He nearly fell asleep twice on the drive over. He swore to himself to get some sleep very soon.

He showed his badge to the receptionist, who asked him to have a seat in the lobby. She left him alone waiting in a room of concrete and black leather chairs. It was contemporary in a cold, scientific way that reminded him of a modern art gallery. He checked the text messages on his phone while he waited for her to return.

A few minutes later, the receptionist introduced him to Doctor Parks, the head of the facility. Doctor Jonathan Parks was an older man with thinning gray hair and wire frame glasses. He looked like the stereotypical college professor, thought the Inspector.

"I am Detective Inspector McNair. I need to speak with you if you have a moment."

"Yes Inspector, please come with me to my office where we can talk in private. Can I get you anything, tea, coffee, bottled water?'

"Thank you, no."

Doctor Parks led him down a well-lit corridor to an office that was sparsely furnished except for the bookshelves overloaded with files and binders. The doctor invited him to be seated.

"Doctor Parks, I am sure you are aware of the death of Mr. James Snelling."

"Yes, I am. Bad business I am afraid."

"Yes, I am investigating his death, and I need your assistance."

"Inspector, you can count on my full cooperation."

"I need some information about Mr. Snelling and the research he conducted at this facility."

"He worked with Katie Munro. They worked with a number of species studying animal behavior."

"Is there anyone that may have worked with him that may be able to shed some light on his research here at Westhill?"

"Let me see. If I am not greatly mistaken, I believe he worked closely with Rebecca Martin, a research assistant in the behavioral science laboratory."

"May I speak with her?"

"I don't see why not. I will see if she is available."

Rebecca Martin was a short woman with dark curly hair and an outgoing personality. She welcomed Inspector McNair into her small, cramped office.

"Inspector, if I can do anything to assist in any way, please let me know," said Doctor Parks as he turned to leave.

"Doctor, can you provide a summary of the research that Mr. Snelling and Mrs. Munro conducted?"

"Of course Inspector, I will have that ready for before you leave," said Doctor Parks as he left Rebecca and the Inspector alone in the tiny room.

"I heard about Mr. Snelling. How sad. He was such a nice guy." She replied, as she took a seat at her diminutive desk and motioned for him to sit down.

"Miss Martin, any information you can provide to me will be a big help. What can you tell me about the research that Mr. Snelling was conducting, particularly on the bats?"

"I hate to tell you this, but not much. I have been busy assisting Doctor Kaplan with his research and was unable to spend much time with Mr. Snelling and Katie. I would help them set up the lab each day and compile data. Mainly, they worked together and rarely needed an assistant."

"What do you know about the bats?"

"Not much about the experiment, but I had to be very careful setting up the lab when Mr. Snelling worked with bats. He was scared to death of them. He insisted that the bats that he worked with always be in cages. At all times. I thought it was a little strange, seeing that he was a vet and a scientist involved in animal research being scared of animals, in particular, bats."

"That is strange. How did you find out he was frightened of bats?"

"Katie, I mean Mrs. Munro told me. I asked her about it one day, I wasn't trying to be rude, I just wanted to know. She told me that he had been attacked by a bat at his office and had developed an irrational fear of them. From what she said, he was scared out of his wits of bats. All I know is that if the animals were not securely contained in a cage, he would get mad at me."

"What about Mr. Snelling? Was he well-liked by his colleagues here at the lab?"

"Oh yes, aside from the bat thing, Mr. Snelling was friendly, nice and had a good sense of humor. I never heard anyone say a bad word about him. I still can't believe he's dead. It just doesn't seem real."

"Rebecca, can you think of anything else about Mr. Snelling or his research that you would like to tell me?"

The young woman seemed to be deep in thought. She finally shook her head and said, "No, nothing else comes to mind."

Inspector McNair remembered what Diane had said earlier that morning, "Have you or anyone here at the laboratory received any threats or has there been any acts of violence or vandalism?"

"Funny you should ask that that. We have received some hate mail lately."

"Do you still have it?"

"I don't know why I kept it, but I have it right here. I suppose I didn't throw it away in case something happened. It seems rather silly since it's not signed by anyone," Rebecca said as she opened a drawer in her desk. She pulled out a small stack of letters and handed them to the Inspector.

"Miss Martin, do you mind if I take these with me? I want to have someone look at them."

"No, I don't mind at all. I feel better knowing you have them and maybe can do something about them. I don't know why we keep getting those letters. This facility researches animal behavior. We don't harm them or anything. The animals here are lazy, well-fed and spoiled. I can show you if you want to see them."

"Some other time perhaps, Miss Martin. You have been very helpful. If you recall any more details that may help with this investigation, please do not hesitate to contact me," he said as he handed her a card.

He slipped the letters into his pocket. They had already been handled and contaminated, but they may still prove to be useful. He returned to Doctor Park's office. The Doctor had a file waiting for him with all the information he had requested. He thanked the Doctor and rushed to his car. He was impatient to get back to the Glen Gorm Hotel.

Chapter 9

It was late in the afternoon when the Inspector returned to the hotel. He walked through the lobby and searched for Diane. He found her on the terrace having tea. He did not wait for the invitation; this time he walked straight to her table.

"Are you expecting anyone?"

"Only you, Inspector. I should have known you would find me out here having tea."

"Inspector Dimbleby, if I didn't know any better, I would say you were teasing me," he said in jest. He knew that he was not supposed to be calling her Inspector, but that was their little joke; besides, he reasoned she would have made a brilliant detective.

"I would say you are right, I have a feeling your afternoon was productive."

"That is one way of putting it," he said as he sat down.

He told Diane about his visit to the lab and the hate mail, and Mr. Snelling's irrational fear of bats. She listened attentively and then made a suggestion, "Have you searched Simon Berry's room?"

"Yes, his room has been searched. Why do you ask?"

"The letters, are they handwritten, or printed from a copier?"

"They appear to be handwritten, do you think there may be a connection?'

"Do you have a sample of Simon's writing? If not, I would think that a search of his room might turn one up."

"Diane, what would I do without you?" he said as he stood up from the table, "I know what I will be doing the rest of the day."

The Inspector inquired at the front desk about the current whereabouts of Mr. Berry. The manager thought he was in his room. The Inspector went upstairs, accompanied by a young sergeant on the police force. The Inspector knocked on the door.

"Who is it? I'm busy," said a voice on the other side of the door.

"Inspector McNair."

The Inspector was certain he heard a few expletives as Simon opened the door, "With all due respect, you have already trashed my room once, what do you want now?"

The Inspector and the Sergeant entered the room. He did a quick look around the room and walked to the desk, "These journals, do they belong to you?" he said as he picked one up, "Is the writing in this journal your writing?"

"Yes, they are my journals, and that's my handwriting. Why do you ask?"

"I need to look at them." The Inspector flipped through the pages of the journal he held in his hand. He removed a piece of hate mail from his pocket and compared the writing. It was an exact match.

"Mr. Berry, can you tell me why your handwriting is on these letters addressed to Westhill Research Laboratory in Inverness?"

Simon Berry said nothing; he sighed and looked down at the ground.

"Sergeant Campbell, arrest this man on a charge of murder and communicating threats. Make arrangements to transport him to Inverness."

Simon Berry was in shock and stared blankly at the Inspector and the Sergeant as his rights were read to him. He did not fight or resist arrest. The Sergeant handcuffed him and led him out of the room. The

Inspector called his team to secure Simon Berry's room and collected evidence.

Inspector McNair yawned as he waited for his team to arrive. He was exhausted and could not remember the last time he had slept for more than a few fitful hours. Now that it looked like he had this case wrapped up, he was looking forward to a long night's sleep.

Chapter 10

Diane was enjoying the summer weather on the terrace in the company of her good friends, Malcolm and Juliana, at the historic Glen Gorm Hotel. It was the holiday she had dreamed of all winter long. After the murder was solved and the killer arrested, she was finally enjoying every second of it.

Diane never intended to spend her summer holiday engaged in amateur sleuthing. Trying to discover the identity of a killer was not on the original itinerary, but it would be a holiday that she was not likely to forget soon. She sipped her tea and felt the sun shine down on her face as Malcolm finished a comical story. It was about the exploits of a drunken guest from America who thought he was Henry the Eighth reincarnated.

"I tell you, Diane, I almost hated to call the police on the man, but he was getting a bit loud with the 'off with her head' remarks," said Malcolm as he reached for a scone.

"Juliana, surely it could not have been as bad as that?" Diane asked.

Juliana answered, "I am afraid he is not exaggerating, that was the craziest story we had about this place up until this murder. I am glad that it is all over now."

"I still cannot believe that Simon was hiding in Mr. Snelling's room, waiting for the perfect moment to blow the whistle. What a frightful scene that must have been, with Mr. Snelling terrified of bats," said Malcolm.

"Can you imagine how frightened he must have been? I'm glad Simon has been arrested." Juliana shuddered, despite the warm weather, "Those last few minutes of his life must have been horrifying."

Diane listened to Malcolm and Juliana discuss the outcome of the police investigation and was struck by a thought that was unsettling. How did Simon know that Mr. Snelling was scared of bats? How would he have known to use a whistle designed specifically for calling that one animal, the only one Mr. Snelling was irrationally afraid of? It did seem rather odd that a stranger would assume a veterinarian would be afraid of animals. The fact that he guessed the exact species was possibly a coincidence, but seemed highly unlikely.

After tea, Diane was unable to relax. She had a nasty suspicion that there was more to this case than she or the Inspector originally thought. She had a feeling that the case was not closed, but was still unsolved. Pulling her phone from her pocket, she powered it on and punched in the code. She scrolled down and found the Inspector's number and texted him.

Call me when you can. Important.

Important? Are you okay?

Yes, case not closed.

The phone buzzed less than ten seconds later. She answered it and was greeted by an Inspector who did not seem happy that she was even suggesting that his case was not as closed as he had hoped. She apologized and requested photos from the wedding that the Munros had attended, all of the photos that could be found. The Inspector reluctantly agreed.

There was nothing left to do but wait patiently for the photographs from the wedding in Mallaig. Less than an hour before, she had been perfectly relaxed enjoying a summer's afternoon in the company of friends. Now, she was back in work mode, thinking about any clue that she may have missed and wondering who might be responsible for the death of Mr. Snelling if it was not Simon.

After tea, she decided to take a walk around the grounds to clear her mind. The police believed that they had the suspect in custody and cleared the guests and staff to leave the premises. Diane wondered if a killer had already left the hotel thinking he had gotten away with murder, or if he was now able to relax and enjoy his holiday.

The walk along the paths that overlooked the ocean gave her an appetite. She returned to the hotel, showered and dressed for dinner. The cook made a delightful roast chicken for dinner, and Diane enjoyed a drink in the lounge with Malcolm and Juliana before retiring for the evening. Later in her room, she checked her phone for messages and saw that there was none. She turned off the light and closed her eyes.

The next morning, she was up early. She was deciding what to wear when her phone buzzed. She had a text message from Inspector McNair.

Will be by later today, will you be available?

Yes.

See you around 3:00

That was quick, she thought to herself as she chose khaki capris and a coral button-down top. The coral was a bright color that complimented her complexion. She dressed and went down to breakfast. There must be something that she could do to try to keep her mind occupied until the Inspector arrived. She settled on working on her novel as the perfect way to pass the time.

Inspector McNair was punctual. He arrived just as Diane was walking downstairs in the lobby. Juliana was working at the front desk since it was the manager's day off. She looked at Diane with a quizzical look on her face, but was quick to volunteer the hotel office for the use of Diane and the Inspector.

"Inspector, I was not expecting a response so quickly," said Diane as they entered the office.

"Neither was I. I was able to contact the official wedding photographer who proved to be extremely helpful."

"Were you able to find any more pictures?"

"Yes, I do have more on the way from several of the guests, but they may take more time. The pictures that the photographer sent seem to be an extensive catalog of the day's activities."

The Inspector handed the large manila envelope to Diane. She opened it and discovered a large stack of pictures, all the size of a standard piece of copy paper. The large size of the pictures made searching for clues much easier, and she was pleasantly surprised to see a time and date recorded on each photograph. She organized the pictures on the desk in chronological order.

"Diane, I have to admit that I was reluctant to request the photos, but your insight into this case has proven to be invaluable. I apologize if I sounded rude on the phone; I was disappointed when you suggested that this case may not be closed."

"Inspector, I assure you that I did not give it a moment's thought. I have been too busy wondering about Simon and the bats. In hindsight, that does seem like a peculiar fact to know about someone, that they are scared of a certain thing or in this case, animal. He would have to have known Mr. Snelling personally, and aside from sending the lab where he worked several threatening letters, I do not see any other connection."

"At least I have managed to solve the mystery of the poison pen letters. That has to be an accomplishment," said the Inspector with a smile.

Diane finished laying out the pictures and began examining each one. The wedding pictures seemed to show a typical wedding; there was the radiant bride and the handsome groom dressed in their finery. There were the guests at the wedding posing with the happy couple. The pictures captured the wedding dinner and the reception, the bride's first dance with her husband and the throwing of the bouquet.

Everything seemed to be in order. The photographer had not missed a moment, not a single detail. Diane was impressed with the angles and lighting the photographer used. He seemed very talented and well-suited for his job. She looked at the pictures for any clues. There was nothing odd or missing, except for one small detail that seemed to be out of place. The Munros were not in any of the pictures after the wedding.

Now that she realized they were missing, it was obvious. She examined every picture of the dinner, reception, and dancing after the ceremony. Peering into the background of the photographs, she looked for even the smallest hint of their presence, but there was nothing. These pictures, she decided, would be a good place to start, and other pictures of the wedding would probably confirm what she was beginning to realize - that they were not at the reception or the dinner.

If they were not in the pictures, then where could they be?

"Inspector, I wonder if you would consider checking these photographs for me. I want to be certain before I arrive at a conclusion."

Inspector McNair stood beside her at the table and leaned closer to Diane to see the pictures that were on the desk.

"I do not see the Munros in any of the pictures after the wedding. I have looked closely, and I don't even see them in the background," she said.

"Let me have a look," he replied as he scrutinized each picture.

He looked at some of the pictures more than once, and finally came to the last pictures, taken at the end of the wedding, a series of group photos, "Here they are; if you look at the front row of these pictures, you will see the Munros standing side by side."

Diane looked at the last photos and saw the Munros smiling at the camera, "Inspector, there is photographic evidence and witness statements placing the Munros at the wedding, and there is photographic evidence that they were present at the end of the evening. My question is where are they between this photograph here, at the wedding, and this group photograph at the end of the night?"

"It does seem strange that they are missing from each picture, but it does not prove anything. Maybe the photographer missed them."

"Inspector, do you honestly believe that they were somehow missing from every picture, even the background?"

"No, I don't believe that, I am only thinking about proof. Where is the proof of your theory?"

Diane thought about what the Inspector said. She had a hunch that she was on to something, that the Munros were missing from the pictures because they were not at the reception, but where was her proof?

Under the steady gaze of the Inspector, she examined every picture on the desk again, starting with the first picture from the wedding.

She knew she was right, but she could not prove it. Diane was beginning to feel frustrated until she came to the last photos of the evening. Looking at the Munros carefully, she searched for even the tiniest clue that would indicate where they had been for a few hours.

She looked at Katie's hair, and it looked a little less neat than it did earlier, but that could easily be explained. She examined the image of Thomas and spotted a minute detail. He was wearing a kilt made of a distinct tartan. There appeared to be a small tear in the kilt visible in the oversized pictures. It was a small detail, but it was the proof that she needed.

"Inspector, look at the kilt that Thomas is wearing in the earlier pictures from the wedding and then in these at the end of the evening, do you notice anything?"

The Inspector examined the pictures and answered, "There is a rip present in the later pictures that could have happened anywhere."

"Yes, it could have happened anywhere, but it didn't happen just anywhere, it happened right here at the Glen Gorm Hotel. As a matter of fact, it happened upstairs in the attic."

"That is a pretty wild assumption," he said in a good-natured way.

"Not at wild as you might imagine, Inspector."

"Why do you say that?"

"See that tartan he is wearing and that place in the fabric where it has been torn? I happen to be in possession of that exact scrap of tartan, and I found it on a nail in the attic!"

"You do have a good point, but there are a few details that I am missing."

"I am sure those details will not be missing for long. I believe you have the wrong suspect in Inverness Inspector, and the real ones are relaxing at this hotel this very minute."

Inspector McNair looked at the pictures once more before he gathered them into a neat stack and slid them into the manila envelope. He thanked Diane for her brilliant detective work and then called for an officer to be dispatched to the hotel. It would not take long for the officer to arrive.

At the front desk, he asked Juliana about the whereabouts of the Munros. Juliana answered that she could not be certain, but she thought they were in the lounge. A few minutes later an officer arrived, Inspector McNair asked him to wait in the lobby. He then went to the lounge to have a talk with the Munros.

Katie and Thomas were having drinks at a table in the lounge. They did not notice that he was standing in the lounge at first. They were laughing and acting like any other happily married couple on holiday. Thomas saw him first, and his mood changed instantly from jovial to surprised. Katie reacted to Thomas's change in mood and turned to face Inspector McNair with a startled look on her face. They were both able to regain their composure by the time he joined them at their table,

"Mr. and Mrs. Munro, I was wondering if I might have a minute? I would like to have a word," he asked.

Mr. Munro appeared to have gone from surprised to see the Inspector to angry, "We do not mind cooperating with you, but quite frankly, this is becoming ridiculous. I have been plagued with police interrogations since I came down here to assist with your enquiries. Then I am told I cannot leave and am trapped here, then the murderer is caught, and now here you are back again. What do you want now?"

Katie winced when her husband spoke to the Inspector as though he was subordinate. The Inspector noted her reaction to her husband's temper tantrum and decided that she must be accustomed to defending his infantile behavior. The Inspector did not appear to notice her husband's rant and continued to speak to him.

"Would you like to stay in the lounge or go somewhere that we may speak in private?" asked the Inspector.

"Here is fine, just don't take long. We were having a good time, until a little while ago," Thomas Munro said with a scowl.

"I will make this simple for both of you, where were you after the wedding in Mallaig?'

"Inspector, we have gone over this, you have our statements, we were at the reception."

"Mr. Munro, we both know you are lying."

Thomas fumed and turned red in rage. Katie spoke calmly, "Inspector, we attended a wedding in Mallaig, we have proof that we were there."

"Yes and no, Mrs. Munro, I have evidence proving that you were at the wedding and later that evening that you were in the last pictures of the event, but I have seen no evidence whatsoever that suggests that you were anywhere near Mallaig in the hours following the wedding."

Katie looked down at the table, and Thomas appeared as though he could stand up at any moment and hit Inspector McNair, before he answered in a voice that ran cold as ice, "Inspector, that is no concern of ours that you do not have pictures at a wedding."

"Mr. and Mrs. Munro, you may believe that I not only have that as evidence, but I have physical evidence as well."

"That is impossible Inspector, we could never have caught a ferry from Mallaig, come all the way back here and then be back that evening to be in the last pictures. That would be impossible with the ferry schedule."

"Not if you had an alternative means of transportation."

"That still does not prove anything, Inspector. Now if you do not mind, are we finished?"

"Yes, Mr. Munro, we are. I can place you at this hotel with sufficient evidence that I am sure you will be convicted of murder in record time."

"That is ridiculous!" thundered Mr. Munro.

"No, it's not. Your kilt that you wore to the wedding is badly in need of repair. If you are curious about the location of the scrap that got torn off that day you were supposed to be at the wedding, you may be interested to know that I have it."

"What do you mean by this?"

"I mean, Mr. Munro, that I know enough of the details and have the evidence that I need to sink you, but I am giving you an opportunity to cooperate. That will look better for you in a court of law, because make no mistake, I will arrest you both for this crime."

Katie and Thomas looked at each other and the anger that Thomas felt seemed to melt into resignation. His shoulders drooped as he began to tell the Inspector his confession. Katie had chimed in a few of the details before she was weeping uncontrollably in the lounge in front of the other guests. Inspector McNair called the police officer positioned in the lobby to join him in the lounge. A few minutes later, Mr. and Mrs. Munro were sitting in the back of a patrol car with their hands cuffed on the way to Inverness to be charged with murder.

The Inspector needed to return to Inverness to drop the murder charge against Simon and interrogate the Munros. He would then file his report detailing the updated charges in the case. It promised to be a busy night, but he wanted to speak with someone before he left the hotel. He needed to speak with Diane. He texted her from the lobby and she came downstairs immediately.

"Mrs. Dimbleby, I was wondering if you would like to see me to my car?"

"Of course, it's a lovely day, I would love to have an excuse to go outside."

"Good, it will give us an opportunity to talk."

She followed the Inspector outside and asked about the Munros. "What happened to the Munros? Where were they during the reception?"

"May I call you Diane, now that the case is closed?"

"Of course you can."

"Then you may call me Robert."

"Robert," she said as she smiled.

"The Munros are on their way to Inverness to be charged with murder."

"What did you find out?"

"They are guilty and they confessed. You were right about the pictures and the tartan, the whistle and there is more."

"More? How did they do it?"

"They were going through a separation that was very likely going to end in divorce when they decided that the source of all their pain and grief was Mr. Snelling. When they knew that they would be nearby in Mallaig for a wedding, she invited Mr. Snelling, who lived nearby, to stay at the hotel under the assumption that she was renewing her affair with him, which she had stopped due to the divorce. Mr. Snelling came to the hotel. The Munros went to the wedding, then used a power boat that they chartered to get back to the island."

"A boat, that does make sense, a charter boat would solve the transportation problem."

"Yes, it does, and once back on the island they had to move fast. Thomas went upstairs to the attic and trapped bats in the bird cage stolen from Timothy, the parrot. He must have torn his kilt in the attic gathering the bats. He then went outside with the cage and waited outside Mr. Snelling's window."

"Where was Katie during all this?"

"Katie convinced Mr. Snelling that she wanted to renew their affair and came to see him that night when she should have been at the reception. While in his room, she opened the window and blew the whistle repeatedly until the bats were agitated. Her husband released them into the room. She blocked the door preventing Mr. Snelling from escaping. I believe you know the rest: Mr. Snelling died, and they returned to the wedding in time for the last photographs."

"Inspector McNair, I am so pleased you were able to extract a confession from them and this case can be officially considered closed."

"Diane, I would never have been able to solve this case without you."

"Robert, it was no trouble."

"Diane, now that we are no longer investigating a murder, would you like to have dinner with me?"

"Robert, I would love to have dinner with you. But I think my husband Albert might not approve." Diane held up her ring finger.

McNair smiled. "I thought that might have been from your marriage to the detective."

Diane shook her head.

McNair held out his hand and Diane shook it. "It's been a pleasure anyway Diane. You live up to your reputation."

As Robert went to his car for the drive back to Inverness, Diane walked back into the Glen Gorm Hotel and joined her friend Juliana for a well-deserved cup of tea. Diane thought how good it felt to return to normal.

She was just afraid that it would not last long. It never did.

Get Your Free Copy of "Murder at the Inn"

Don't forget to grab your free copy of Penelope Sotheby's first novella *Murder At The Inn* while you still can.

Go to http://fantasticfiction.info/murder-at-the-inn/ to find out more.

Other Books by This Author

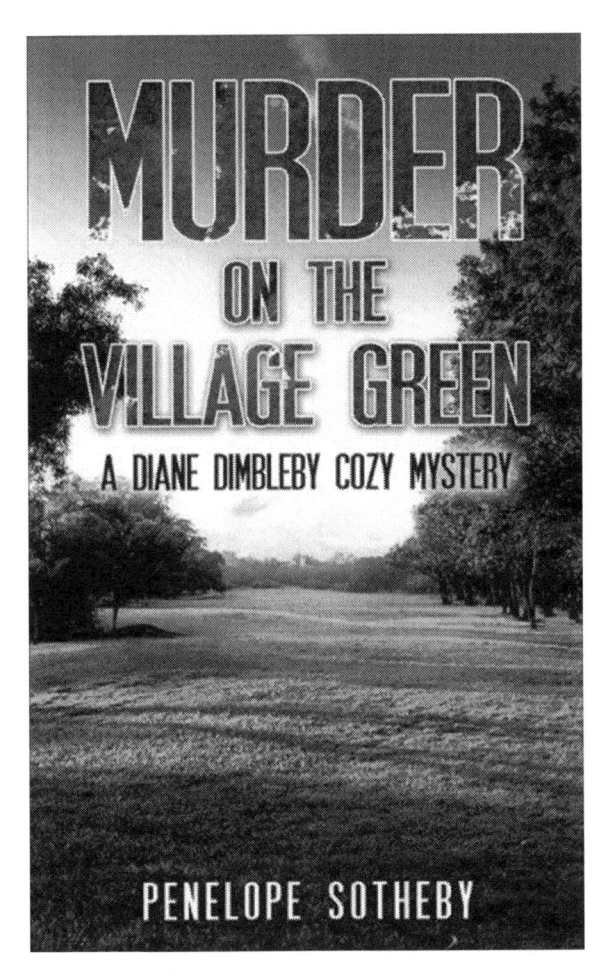

Murder on the Village Green

Murder in the Neighbourhood

Murder on a Yacht

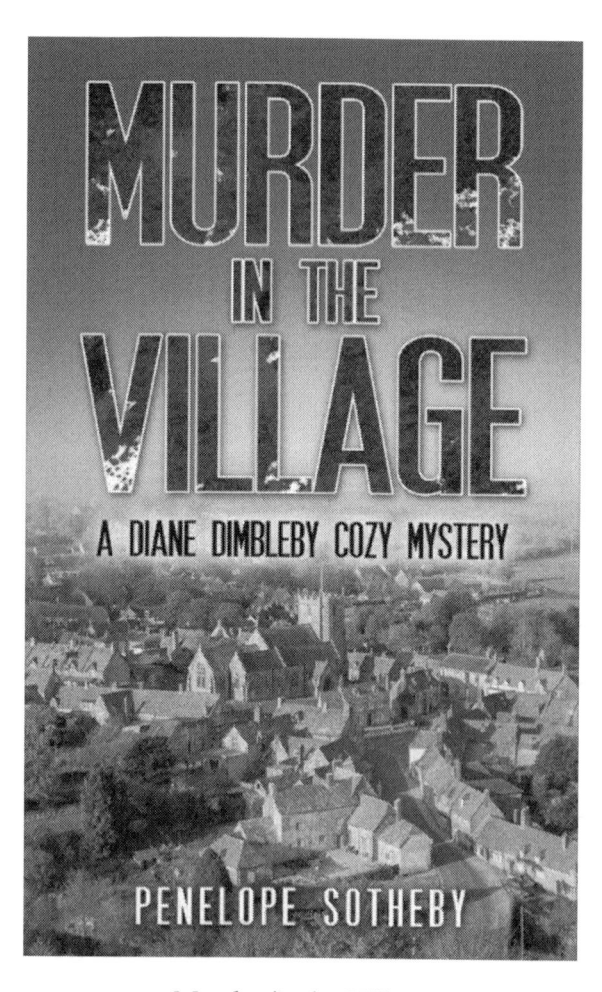

Murder in the Village

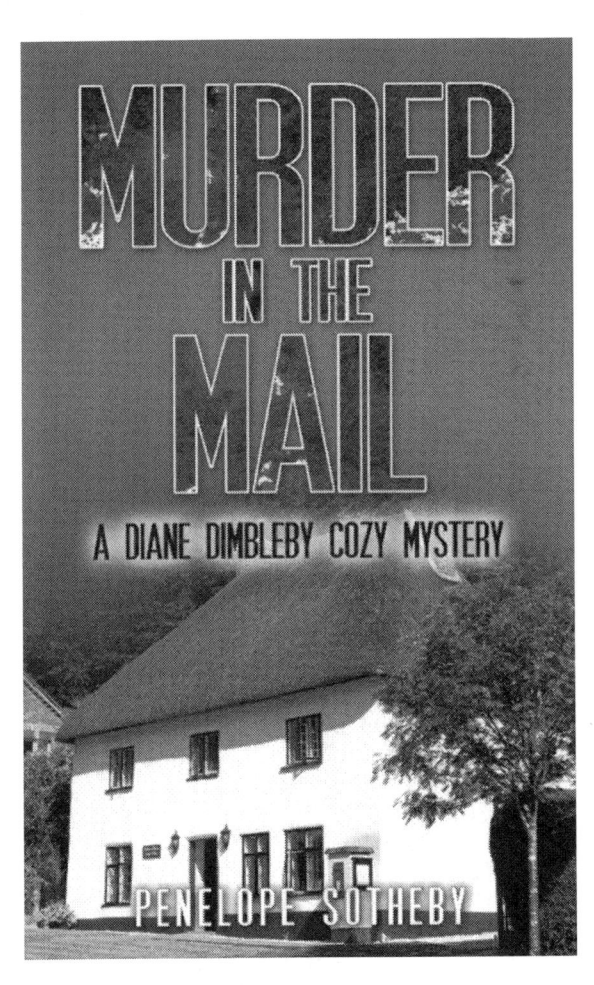

Murder in the Mail

Murder in the Development

About The Author

For many, the thought of childhood conjures images of hopscotch games in quiet neighbourhoods, and sticky visits to the local sweet shop. For Penelope Sotheby, childhood meant bathing in Bermuda, jiving in Jamaica and exploring a string of strange and exotic British territories with her nomadic family. New friends would come and go, but her constant companion was an old, battered collection of Agatha Christie novels that filled her hours with intrigue and wonder.

Penelope would go on to read every single one of Christie's sixty-six novels—multiple times—and so was born a love of suspense than can be found in Sotheby's own works today.

In 2011 the author debuted with *"Murder at the Inn"*, a whodunit novella set on Graham Island off the West Coast of Canada. After receiving positive acclaim, Sotheby went on to write the series *"Murder in Paradise"*; five novels following the antics of a wedding planner navigating nuptials (and crime scenes) in the tropical locations of Sotheby's formative years.

An avid gardener, proud mother, and passionate host of Murder Mystery weekends, Sotheby can often be found at her large oak table, gleefully plotting the demise of her friends, tricky twists and grand reveals.

Fantastic Fiction

Fantastic Fiction publishes short reads that feature stories in a series of five or more books. Specializing in genres such as Mystery, Thriller, Fantasy and Sci Fi, our novels are exciting and put our readers at the edge of their seats.

Each of our novellas range around 20,000 words each and are perfect for short afternoon reads. Most of the stories published through Fantastic Fiction are escapist fiction and allow readers to indulge in their imagination through well written, powerful and descriptive stories.

Why Fiction?

At Fantastic Fiction, we believe that life doesn't get much better than kicking back and reading a gripping piece of fiction. We are passionate about supporting independent writers and believe that the world should have access to this incredible works of fiction. Through our store we provide a diverse range of fiction that is sure to satisfy.

www.fantasticfiction.info

Made in the USA
Columbia, SC
17 September 2018